# PUZZLE CASTLE

## Susannah Leigh

## Illustrated by Brenda Haw

## Designed by Paul Greenleaf

# Contents

Series Editor: Gaby Waters

# About this book

This book is about a brave knight called Sophie and her adventure at Puzzle Castle. There is a puzzle on every double page. Solve them all and help Sophie on her way. If you get stuck, look at the answers on pages 31 and 32.

This is Sophie, the brave knight. She lives in a village not far from Puzzle Castle.

This is Puzzle Castle.

Sophie's friend, Titus the Timid, lives in Puzzle Castle. He has written Sophie a letter. Here it is.

This is Titus. He is wearing his banquet outfit.

Puzzle Castle
Monday

Dear Sophie,

You are invited to a grand banquet in Puzzle Castle today, but first we need your help. For the past three days there has been a monster in the dungeons. No one has seen it, but everyone is very scared. You are the bravest person I know. Could you come early and get rid of it? I will meet you in the castle courtyard at three o'clock.

Love from your friend, Titus.

P.S. I will be wearing my banquet outfit!

## Useful equipment

When Sophie gets to the castle she will need to find ten things that may come in handy when she reaches the dungeons. You will find one object on every double page, from the moment she enters the castle, until she arrives at the monster's lair...

umbrella

powerful flashlight

monster protection shield

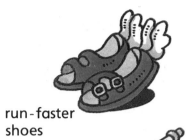
run-faster shoes

monster phrase book

monster protection helmet

key

mystery box

extra-brave toffees

useful string

## Cecil the castle ghost

Puzzle Castle is haunted by a very friendly ghost. His name is Cecil. He is hiding spookily on every double page. See if you can spot him.

## Jester Jim

Jester Jim is practising his juggling for the banquet, but he's not very good at it. He has lost his juggling balls around the castle. There is at least one hiding on every double page.
Can you find them?

The juggling balls look like this.

3

# The adventure starts

On the day of the grand banquet, Sophie set out for Puzzle Castle. As she drew near, the castle loomed ahead of her, surrounded by a monstrous moat. Peering down into the water she saw strange creatures and big fish with snappy teeth.

The only way across the water was by the many bridges. But this wasn't as easy as it looked. Some of the bridges were broken and others were too dangerous to cross. Sophie would have to be very careful.

**Can you find a safe route across the moat?**

# Where is Titus?

Sophie jumped to the safety of the bank. She bounded up to the castle gate and pulled the bell which jangled loudly. The gate rose slowly and Sophie stepped into the bustling courtyard of Puzzle Castle.

Everyone was busy preparing for the grand banquet and trying hard not to think about the monster in the dungeons. It was nearly three o' clock. Sophie looked out for Titus. She was sure he was hiding somewhere.

**Can you see Titus?**

# Sophie's instructions

"Don't worry, Titus, I'll deal with the monster," said Sophie bravely. "Lead me to the dungeons."

"Oh no, Sophie," Titus shivered. "You are brave enough to find the monster by yourself. Here's a plan of Puzzle Castle, and a list of people you will meet on your journey. You must visit each person in turn. Each one needs your help getting ready for the banquet. Help them out and you will soon find your way to the dungeons."

**Can you match the people with the rooms where Sophie is most likely to find them?**

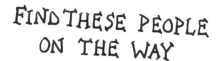

## FIND THESE PEOPLE ON THE WAY

MERVIN, Portrait Keeper

PRINCESS POSY

LARRY, Look-out boy

BETH the Babysitter

MRS. CRUMB the Cook

WIZARD WILF

8

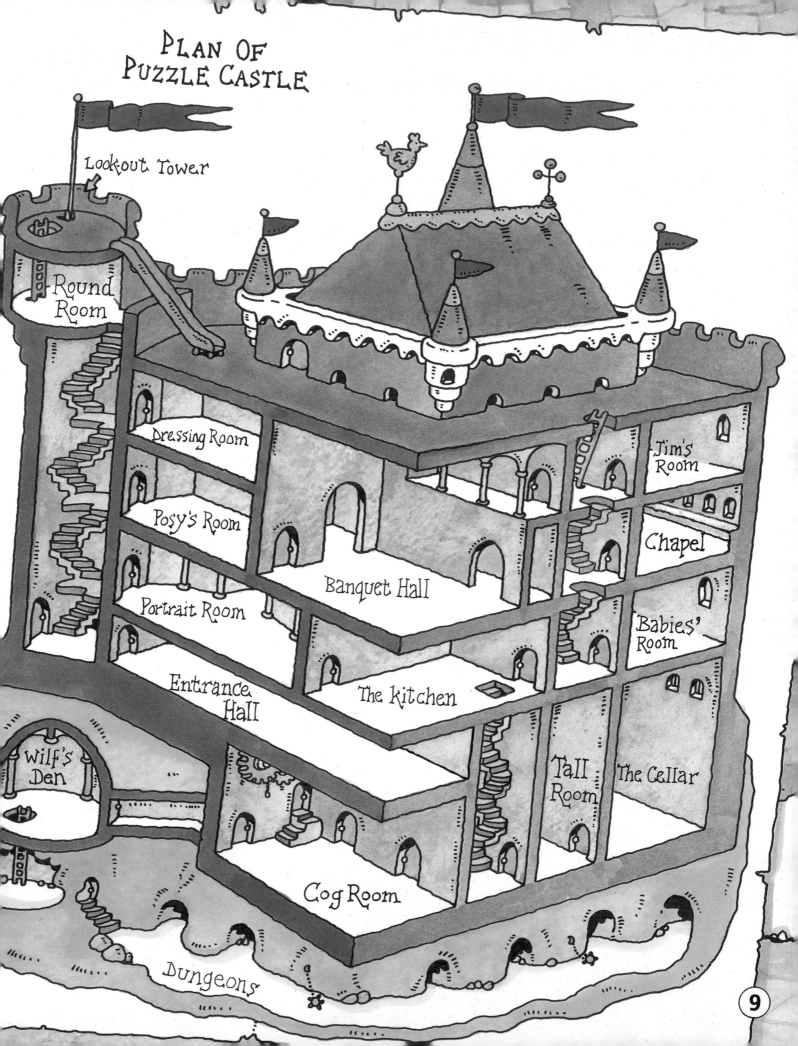

PLAN OF
PUZZLE CASTLE

Lookout Tower

Round Room

Dressing Room

Posy's Room

Portrait Room

Entrance Hall

Banquet Hall

The Kitchen

Jim's Room

Chapel

'Babies' Room

Tall Room

The Cellar

Wilf's Den

Cog Room

Dungeons

# Royal portraits

Sophie promised to see Titus later and began her journey. Her first stop was the portrait gallery.

"Sophie," cried Mervin the portrait keeper. "Princess Posy's Uncle Edwin is coming all the way from Gruldavia for the banquet. I have to meet him, but I've forgotten what he looks like. If I get this wrong, I'll be thrown in the dungeons. His picture is here. He has black hair, a beard and a moustache. He always wears red and purple. He has no children and he doesn't like horses."

**Can you find Uncle Edwin's picture?**

Does Uncle Edwin have big ears?

# Princess Posy's problem

Sophie curtsied as she entered Princess Posy's room. What a mess it was!

"Sophie!" cried Posy. "I know you're going to fight the monster, but I've got a bigger problem. I want to wear my matching necklace, bracelet, ring and crown to the banquet. I can't find them in my big wooden chest."

**Can you find a necklace, a bracelet, a ring and a crown that match?**

# The look-out tower

Sophie left Posy admiring her jewels, and climbed up to the castle battlements. Here she found Larry the look-out boy, pointing to a lot of people approaching the castle.

"Sophie!" he cried. "All these people are arriving for the grand banquet, but I don't know if they've been invited."

**Banquet guest list**

BARON BORIS the BAD and his BADDIES (not invited - deserves 3 bad eggs)

SIR HORACE and his HORRIBLES (not invited - deserves soup treatment)

SIR NICE NED and his FRIENDS (invited)

COUNT CURTIS and his CRAFTY COUSINS (not invited - bubbling treacle treatment)

LADY LUCY LOVELY and FRIENDS (invited)

FEARLESS FREDA and FRIENDS (invited)

WONDERFUL WANDA and her FRIENDS (invited)

NASTY KNIGHT KEVIN and NASTIES (not invited - aim rubber arrows at him)

BAD EGGS

DUNG

SOUP

BUBBLING TREACLE

Sophie read the guest list. Then she looked at the flags of the approaching groups and checked to see if they were invited or not.

**Do you know who is invited to the banquet?**

# Beth and the babies

Sophie scrambled down to the babies' room. Here she found Beth, the very new babysitter, and lots of naughty babies.

"Sophie," cried Beth. "I have to dress the babies for the banquet, but I don't know which clothes belong to which baby. I've even forgotten each baby's name!"

Sophie looked at the party outfits hanging on the wall. Then she looked at the babies in their underwear. Soon she had matched them together.

**Can you find the right outfit for each baby?**

# In the kitchen

Sophie left Beth with the smartly dressed babies and followed the smell of burnt banquet buns to the kitchen. The grand banquet feast was boiling away, but Mrs. Crumb the cook was flustered.

"I wanted to make you a monster-fighting pudding to build up your strength, Sophie," she said. "But some rascal has hidden the ingredients. I've lost two red plums, a pot of honey, three fresh eggs, four loaves of bread and a lemon."

**Can you find the missing pudding ingredients?**

19

# Which way now?

"I'll have to eat that pudding later!" Sophie called, as she dropped through the trapdoor. She climbed down some steep steps. To the right was a door. She pushed it open and walked into a room with cogs hanging from the ceiling. There was no one here, so Sophie decided to move on.

Her next stop was Wizard Wilf's den. But which door led to it? There were six to choose from, but danger lurked behind almost every one. Sophie looked at her castle plan and soon knew which door to take.

**Which door should Sophie choose?**

# The wizard's den

Sophie pushed open the door and walked down a small passageway to another door. Through this door lay Wizard Wilf's secret den. Wilf stood stirring a big pot.

"Sophie," he cried. "I'm brewing a magic potion to cast a spell. It will make you invisible and help you dodge the monster."

Sophie held her breath as Wilf waved his magic wand. There was a purple flash and a puff of smoke, but when it had cleared they saw the spell hadn't quite worked. Sophie was still there, but lots of other things had vanished.

**How many things have disappeared?**
**Can you spot them all?**

After...

Witch Hazel

bananas

My pets

101 BEST SPELLS

MAGIC POWDER

useful bones

# Sophie finds the way

There was no time to waste. Sophie climbed down Wilf's ladder and crept along an underground passageway. She soon found herself at the beginning of a maze of tunnels. In the distance she could hear the terrible roars of the monster. She didn't want to get lost underground as she made her way towards the roars, so she unravelled her ball of useful string as she went.

**Can you find the way to the monster's roars?**

25

# The monster's lair...

The rumbling and roaring noise grew louder as Sophie reached the end of the maze. She was at the top of a small flight of steps.

Sophie checked she had all her equipment with her. Chewing nervously on an extra-brave toffee, Sophie began her final journey, down the winding staircase to the monster's lair...

Water dripped down.

It was very dark.

She buckled her special run-faster shoes.

She put on her helmet and shield.

She checked her monster phrase book.

She turned the key.

Where's the station?

*Zip zap zop?*

Hello. Are you a friendly monster?

*Og gob glook?*

She opened the door and saw...

...a little dragon, crying and sniffing. Was this the fierce monster of Puzzle Castle? Could Sophie cheer him up?

Hello ... hic ... sob. My name's Dennis. I got stuck in this scary dungeon. I'm hungry and cold and I've lost my mum.

Then she remembered. She could give him the one piece of equipment she hadn't used yet.

**What can Sophie give Dennis?**

# The grand banquet

Dennis cheered up at once. Then Sophie had another idea. She would take him to the banquet. Sophie led Dennis back through the castle and up to the grand banquet hall.

At first everyone was scared of Dennis. But they soon saw he wasn't a monster at all. He was a very friendly little dragon who liked to dance. Everyone was very pleased to see him.

**There is someone in this picture who is especially happy to see Dennis. Do you know who it is?**

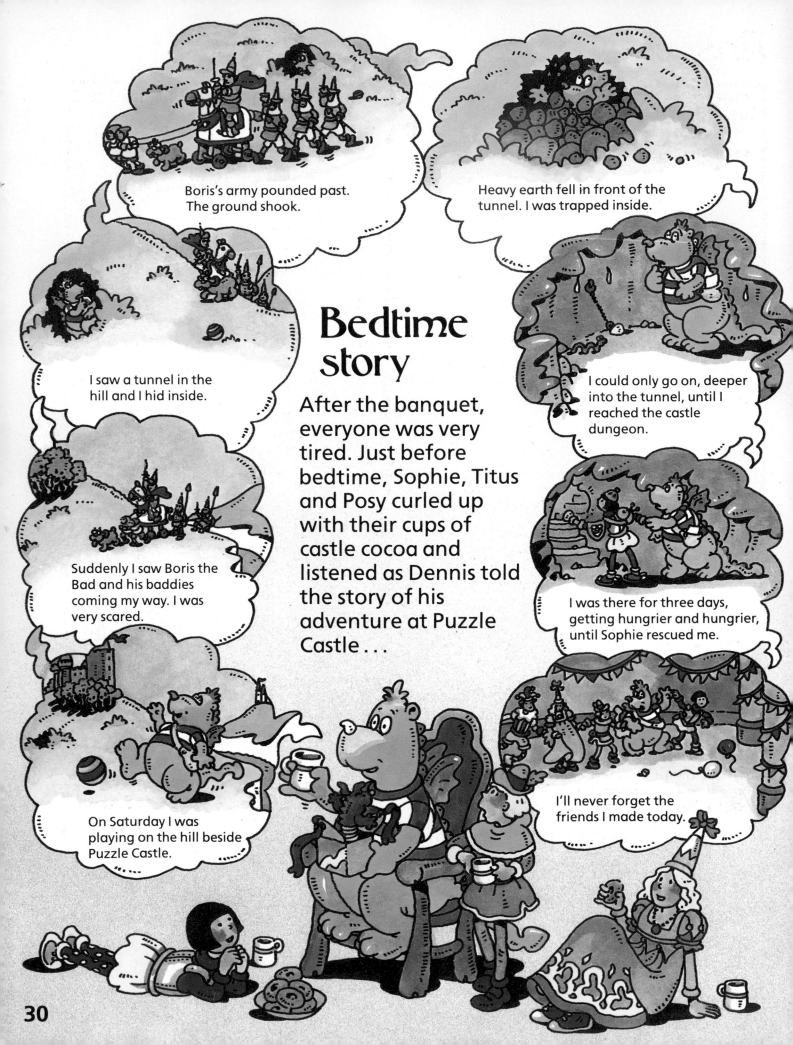

# Bedtime story

Boris's army pounded past. The ground shook.

Heavy earth fell in front of the tunnel. I was trapped inside.

I saw a tunnel in the hill and I hid inside.

I could only go on, deeper into the tunnel, until I reached the castle dungeon.

After the banquet, everyone was very tired. Just before bedtime, Sophie, Titus and Posy curled up with their cups of castle cocoa and listened as Dennis told the story of his adventure at Puzzle Castle . . .

Suddenly I saw Boris the Bad and his baddies coming my way. I was very scared.

I was there for three days, getting hungrier and hungrier, until Sophie rescued me.

On Saturday I was playing on the hill beside Puzzle Castle.

I'll never forget the friends I made today.

# Answers

## Pages 4-5 The adventure starts

The route to the castle is shown in red.

## Pages 6-7 Where is Titus?

Titus is here.

## Pages 8-9 Sophie's instructions

| Person | Room |
|---|---|
| Mervin | Portrait Room |
| Princess Posy | Posy's Room |
| Larry | Look-out Tower |
| Beth | Babies' Room |
| Mrs. Crumb | Kitchen |
| Wizard Wilf | Wilf's Den |

## Pages 10-11 Royal portraits

This is Uncle Edwin.

## Pages 12-13 Princess Posy's problem

Posy's matching jewels are circled in red.

## Pages 14-15 The look-out tower

Lady Lucy Lovely, Sir Nice Ned and Fearless Freda are all invited to the banquet. Baron Boris the Bad and his baddies aren't invited.

## Pages 16-17 Beth and the babies

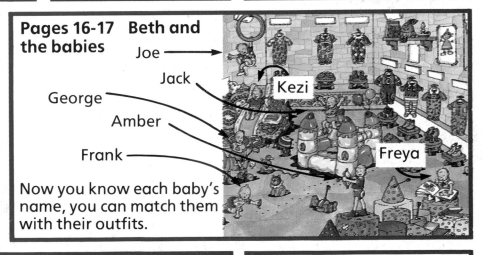

Joe
Jack
Kezi
George
Amber
Freya
Frank

Now you know each baby's name, you can match them with their outfits.

## Pages 18-19 In the kitchen

The missing ingredients are circled in red.

## Pages 20-21 Which way now?

Sophie should go through this door.

## Pages 22-23
### The wizard's den
The red circles show where Wilf's things were.

## Pages 24-25
### Sophie finds the way
The way to the monster is shown in red.

## Pages 26-27   The monster's lair...
Sophie gives Dennis the mystery box she found in the wizard's den. It is a dragon-in-a-box!

## Pages 28-29   The grand banquet
Dennis's mum is especially happy to see him. Here she is.

# Did you spot everything?

### Juggling balls

### Useful equipment

### Cecil the ghost

The chart below shows you how many juggling balls are hidden on each double page. You can also find out which piece of Sophie's useful equipment is hidden where.

Did you remember to look out for Cecil the ghost? He is hiding spookily on every double page. Look back through the book again and see if you can find him.

| Pages | Juggling balls | Useful equipment |
|---|---|---|
| 4-5 | one | none here! |
| 6-7 | four | monster protection shield |
| 8-9 | one | key |
| 10-11 | three | useful string |
| 12-13 | four | run-faster shoes |
| 14-15 | two | umbrella |
| 16-17 | three | monster phrase book |
| 18-19 | five | extra-brave toffees |
| 20-21 | two | monster protection helmet |
| 22-23 | three (or is it six?) | mystery box |
| 24-25 | four | powerful flashlight |
| 26-27 | one | none here! |
| 28-29 | nineteen | none here! |

This edition first published in 2003 by Usborne Publishing Ltd., Usborne House, 83-85 Saffron Hill, London EC1N 8RT, England.

www.usborne.com Copyright © 2003, 1992 Usborne Publishing Ltd.

The name Usborne and the devices ♀ ⊕ are Trade Marks of Usborne Publishing Ltd.

Printed in Portugal.